Published by

Bullfinch Books.
Scottish Provident Building, 7 Donegall Square West, Belfast, BT1 6JH
Bullfinch Books is a trading name of Voz Media Ltd.

Printed in China
ISBN: 978-1-5272-2171-0

Order from **worldatyourfeet.co**

WORLD at your FEET

by **Rob Parker**

Illustrated by **Lawerta**

Leap like a salmon, control on your chest,
It's time to become the world's very best.

Over a defender you flick the ball,
It's up in the sky... will it ever fall?

Time moves slowly, you get yourself set.
Tick-tock, tick-tock, the ball is in the net.

A cannonball launched,
it's barely in sight,
Tiptoe the line between shadow and light.

Some magical control brings the ball under your spell,
A sneaky second touch beats the defender as well.

Out of the shade and run into the sun,
An elegant flick and the game is won.

A creepy-crawly spider
asleep on the grass.
A flick, twist and turn,
and two defenders you pass.
You're like a turbo-charged lamb
as you leap past two more.
From halfway line to six-yard box,
now a chance to score.

You go around the keeper,
and there's no stopping you now.
Fire the ball into the goal.
There's no other word but wow!

A team-mate spots your run and passes the ball there.
You let it roll onto your foot and flick it in the air,
Then spin around and kick it like you're doing taekwondo.

There's only one place the ball is ever going to go.
It nestles just inside the post, in the corner of the net.
Mouth open, arms outstretched, like you can't believe it yet.

You hurdle past the first man, run then skip inside.
A defender flies past you with a misjudged slide.

You've made it this close to goal by working all alone,
Can you now finish the job
and score all on your own?

Kick the ball past a defender,
run onto your own pass,
And lift it past the keeper
with another touch of class.

A huge, floating cross,
the ball will land in space.

You and the defenders
are going to have a race.

Your run is perfect,
so you don't break the offside rule.

You dive at the ball
like a belly flop in the pool.

Head meets ball, and you nod it above the goalkeeper's reach.

Ball meets net as you meet ground,
like a whale stuck on a beach.

You're on the halfway line.
What are you going to do?
Pass to a team-mate, and he passes back to you.

Run towards goal,
a player lunges at your feet,

But you skip past the tackle
and leave him on his seat.

A dance floor shimmy gets the next man in a tangle.
You curl the ball into the goal at the perfect angle.

A clever little swivel
gives you time and space.
You're past one defender,
beat the next one for pace.

You gallop at goal,
like a determined gazelle,
Then you smash the ball
straight past the keeper as well.

After scoring a great goal you've earned a short break.
Run to the corner flag for a wiggle and shake.

Pass the ball, pass the ball, move it up the pitch.
From yellow shirt to yellow shirt.
But wait, is this a glitch?
A pass that's made to no-one,
the ball rolls into space.
You appear from nowhere
and to the ball you race.

You kick it really hard with not a moment to think.
It zooms from foot to goal in the time it takes to blink.

Your team has got the ball
and they pass it everywhere.
Lots of players get a kick (because it's nice to share).

You pass it to a team-mate,
who does a sneaky trick

And gives it back to you
with a nifty little flick.

You don't need to pass this time, you slide to score the goal,
And though you got the final touch, they all played their role.

A motorcycle kickstart flicks the ball past your man.
On your bike and head for goal as quickly as you can.

He nearly catches up with you,
but you're strong as well as fast,
You've beaten one defender,
but can you make it past the last?

You run rings around him like you're on a cartoon show,
Then clip the ball into the goal. "Sorry, guys, too slow!"

The ball is passed to you... or will it go to your team-mate?
It rolls between his legs, like a sheep going through a gate.

When the ball arrives you greet it with a teeny-tiny flick,
And before it has time to bounce, you give it another kick.
This one's not teeny-tiny, it's a super-duper blast.
And it soars into the net while the keeper stands aghast.

WOW!

Juggling outside the penalty box,
trying to make the right connection,
Flick the ball to a team-mate,
who sends it back in your direction.

You throw your body through the air
as the ball returns to you.
Is this football or gymnastics?
Or perhaps it is kung-fu.

Floating above the ground,
an acrobatic pose.
A horizontal volley.
Into the goal it goes.

A team-mate heads the ball forward, you control it on your chest.
Send a message to the world: "Prepare to be impressed."

In the same movement, you somehow swivel around,
Then kick the ball sweetly before it's hit the ground.

The ball flies off your boot, the keeper can't get near,
Off the crossbar, into the goal and the crowd starts to cheer.

Neat passing in the box and your team's on the attack.
Then somewhat unexpectedly, the ball is passed back.
You control the ball away from you to make a bit of space,
(At this point you score the goal, but this tale's about your face).

On the stretch you find the net. Should you laugh or should you cry?
Pumping arms and screams of joy, and the stadium rushing by.

One more goal to make sure that your team wins the cup.
You run towards the box, the defender backing up.
Is this the perfect end to this sunny afternoon?
Some fans are on the pitch, they're celebrating too soon.
Whack the ball into the net with a mighty POW!
They think it's all over and - guess what - it is now.